ACCEPTING LOVE

CONNOR WHITELEY

No part of this book may be reproduced in any form or by any electronic or mechanical means. Including information storage, and retrieval systems, without written permission from the author except for the use of brief quotations in a book review.

This book is NOT legal, professional, medical, financial or any type of official advice.

Any questions about the book, rights licensing, or to contact the author, please email connorwhiteley@connorwhiteley.net

Copyright © 2024 CONNOR WHITELEY

All rights reserved.

DEDICATION

Thank you to all my readers without you I couldn't do what I love.

CHAPTER 1
15th March 2023
Canterbury, England

University Psychology Tom Palmer was so excited for tonight as he sat down on the large fabric black sofa that dominated an entire corner of the shared kitchen he had with his flat mates at Kent University. He had no idea who's bright idea it was to have such a massive sofa completely taking up a corner, but it could have been worse he supposed.

Tom wasn't sure how it could be worst, because him and his flatmates had very quickly realised whoever had the bottom draw in the bright silver fridge-freezer was going to have a hell of a job getting to their food, considering the gap between the freezer door and the end of the sofa was so small it was flat out impossible to open the door completely.

Besides from that, Tom had to admit that this was one of the best kitchens he'd seen around campus. Tom liked the silver cabinets with their weird golden nobs and fake black marble worktops that were really just chipboard.

The large kitchen island that served as a dinner table and somewhere else to prepare food was made from even more of the fake marble chip wood, but it looked good and it served its purpose so Tom supposed it was okay.

He knew that everyone cooking would never happen and Tom had learnt a ton about international eating habits through who used the kitchen when.

His very hot French friend and the Italian girl always cooked dinner together at about 8 pm, whilst the Portuguese guy that Tom avoided like the plague cooked about 10 pm. It was fascinating to see how different cultures prepared and cooked their dinners.

And that was something Tom flat out loved about university.

Tom just smiled to himself as he enjoyed the brief moment of silence. He couldn't deny that was the only problem with living in university halls that the sheer amount of noise at night. It was bad enough when the person above him decided to have sex and Tom could hear the bed move constantly. That was just mortifying.

It was better though than people running up and down the corridors at night at 2 am after returning from a party or something. It was one of the reasons why Tom liked going home in the breaks so he could go to sleep before 2 am. Tom didn't care that it was such a small luxury, he was always going to treasure it.

"Afternoon sunshine," a woman said as she came into the kitchen.

Tom smiled at Jasmine as she came into the kitchen wearing her normal long black tracksuit with her long brown hair flowing by her shoulders and she was grinning like normal. Tom really hoped that her and her boyfriend were getting on better now, because she was definitely too great a woman to not have someone to love.

As Jasmine came over, picked up a jug of orange juice on the side (that had been there for three days) and drank it, Tom just shook his head and enjoyed the sweet aromas of oranges and Lalics and lavender that was definitely coming from Jasmine's perfume that Tom was surprised she didn't drown in half the time. At least it made the great taste of a warm summer picnic form on his tongue like he used to have with his family.

He really needed to do that again at some point but he wouldn't see his family for at least another few weeks during Easter break.

"How's life?" Jasmine asked like she always did when she was trying to ease into wanting something.

As much as Tom wanted to cut to the chase, he really did like Jasmine too much to deny the so-called joy of easing into what she wanted. She was a great listener, a great friend and she really did know how to help out with boys.

"I thought you had a lecture?" Tom asked and he shook his head as Jasmine offered him a drink of juice.

"Like you can talk?"

Tom smiled. She was hardly wrong but his lecture had been moved to the morning when he normally went running, went to the gym with his friends and at times he helped out at a local gay charity helping homeless gay youths.

A charity that Tom really did love working for.

"I asked first," Tom said, sticking his tongue out.

"You know, this is my first year at uni I can do whatever I want and it's more fun spending time with Ben compared to lectures," Jasmine said.

Tom couldn't deny that. As soon as he had learnt that his first year at university wouldn't count towards his final degree classification, he hadn't stopped trying, but he was a lot more relaxed about everything.

"Speaking of which don't you have assignments or something that means you shouldn't be in here?" Jasmine asked.

"Why do I get the feeling that you want to get rid of me?" Tom asked smiling.

"Because I may have asked Ben over and I didn't want you giving him a hard time,"

Tom laughed to himself because he was happy that Ben and Jasmine were together, but he just didn't want to keep having to comfort Jasmine when she was hurt, upset or Ben had said something mean to her.

Thankfully that hadn't happened for months but

Tom also just wanted to sleep before 2 am. It was the main reason why he wanted Ben and Jasmine back together but he wasn't going to tell her that.

Tom hugged her. "As long as he doesn't hurt you I don't care if I see him or not,"

"Thank you," Jasmine said kissing him on the cheek. "Where are you off to tonight?"

Tom grinned. He had been waiting for this all week and he was so damn excited about it.

"So you know I came out to my parents properly last year and I've been taking baby steps towards being gay, being part of the community and so on?"

Jasmine nodded.

"Well tonight all of us student ambassadors as part of the community are actually coming together to make a zine to try and bust the myths about the queer community," Tom said knowing exactly how overexcited he sounded.

"Sorry, um, what's a zine?" Jasmine asked.

Tom shrugged. "I have no idea but that's why I'm going tonight,"

Jasmine nodded. Tom loved it how she was trying to be encouraging but she didn't know how much this meant to him. It wasn't really the making of the zine itself that mattered at all. The point was that he was going to be mixing with other gay people, having fun and having conversations that even a year ago would have been impossible for him to have.

Tom smiled at Jasmine because he could tell she was trying to be as supportive as she possibly could, but he normally had these conversations with his other friends on his psychology course. They actually had an input and something to say.

"Enjoy," Jasmine said as she downed her orange juice and Tom just shook his head.

He couldn't imagine anything worse than drinking three-day-old orange juice but if university wasn't a time to form bad habits, then when in life could you?

CHAPTER 2
15th March 2023
Canterbury, England

University student Henry Burton took a deep breath of the wonderful tomato, basil and cheese-infused air as he sat down in one of Kent University's many cafes and restaurants. He seriously wasn't sure why the university needed so many different places to eat, chat and drink but he was more than happy for it.

Mango's Café was definitely one of the more extreme places to eat on campus, and Henry was surprised he hadn't eaten at it yet, because it was all focused on more wild things to eat.

Henry was really surprised by the impressive design of the small café with its black walls covered with fake plastic leaves, jungle paintings and massive plastic pineapples that covered everything. He sort of felt like he was in a jungle and even the tree bark texture of the tables were certainly different in a good way.

The quiet sound of jungle music made Henry smile because this was a flat out weird place to eat, but it was great to be here. And thankfully there were tons of other people here too.

Two tables away Henry noticed there was a group of sporty university students belonging to the university football team. Henry couldn't help but focus on their board shoulders, strong jawline and beautiful smiles as they started to drink their afternoon away.

Henry wrapped his hands around his tall glass of diet coke as a young waitress walked past him holding three pizzas for the large table behind him.

And Henry just smiled to himself because he was finally out in public as a man. He couldn't help but feel glad that after coming out to his parents as trans last year and slowly encouraging himself over the past few months that he was okay, he could freely dress like a man in public and just be who he really was, that he was finally in public as the person he was meant to be.

As much as Henry would have liked to spend his afternoon helping at the local soup kitchen, doing some Ambassador work so he could inspire more disadvantaged children that they could go to university, or doing something else that helped people like he normally did during the week when he wasn't in lectures. He was glad that his best friend Adam wanted to meet up.

Henry was a little annoyed that he was a little late

but Henry smiled as he realised he had no idea how Adam functioned half the time. It was a joke between Henry and Adam's girlfriend Amy that she basically had to mother him half the time.

It was just a shame that Henry didn't think it was a joke half the time, but he wouldn't change his friendship with Adam for anything.

"Hi," a man said.

Henry smiled at his best friend Adam, wearing his black jeans, blue t-shirt and black baseball cap (a little habit they shared) as he sat down opposite him and ordered a diet coke from the waitress as she walked out.

Henry felt a lot happier now that Adam was here. It felt stupid that he was so nervous but he read the news, he knew what could happen to trans people and this was just all so new to himself.

"You look hot," Adam said.

Henry shook his head because he just didn't sound right coming from Adam's lips. He was perfectly straight, a great friend who had helped him with everything so far but Adam saying that he was hot just didn't sound right at all.

"So how you finding it?" Adam said smiling.

Henry shook his head. "You were late on purpose weren't you?"

Henry loved it how Adam shrugged and he couldn't blame Adam for leaving him alone so he just get used to being in public. He couldn't have cared less about the fact that he was who he was meant to be, but he was paranoid about people looking, judging and making comments.

Or maybe that was just him thinking that because his parents had done it, everyone else was going to do it too.

"Hey, how you finding that thermodynamic essay question?" Adam asked.

Henry was really glad for the change in subject, anything to help him focus on other things.

"It's a tough one when you first look at it but you need to make sure that you don't overthink it," Henry said. "But I know you already know this because you keep getting firsts in all your assignments,"

Adam shrugged. "Guilty is charged. What you up to tonight? Me and Amy are going out with Jordan if you wanted to join us,"

Henry had to admit he did like going out with Jordan, because he was a lot of fun, a great guy to be around and Jordan was hardly bad on the eyes, but Henry was thankfully too busy.

"I can't tonight. I'm working at Outreach event," Henry said.

"Please tell me it's another queer one,"

"Wow," Henry said. "You really want me to get a boyfriend don't you?"

Adam nodded. "Of course I do, and I want you to accept yourself fully in public. I know you're a brilliant person, I know what you're really like but even now I know you're tense,"

Henry looked at the ground. He really didn't

want to admit that he was acting like half a person or not like how Adam knew him.

"I know this is scary and I know you've been through stuff," Adam said knowing Henry wasn't liking this, "but I know the real you and any man that sees this will be lucky to have you,"

Henry smiled. "You really are a great friend,"

Then Henry looked at the time and realised if he was ever going to make the event then he definitely needed to leave sooner rather than later.

He was about to go when Adam gently grabbed his hands. "I meant what I said though. I might be into girls but you really do look beautiful,"

Henry smiled to be nice but just hearing that made him feel weird and awkward but also really hopeful for the future, because if a straight guy like Adam could find him beautiful then maybe a gay guy could too.

And that really would make Henry's year.

CHAPTER 3
15th March 2023

Canterbury, England

Tom wrapped his hands around the large white plastic coffee cup as he took his seat in one of the university's many seminar rooms for the Zine workshop and he was so excited. It was going to be a great night of making friends, talking and just having brilliant conversations that even a year ago he never would have imagined he would be having.

The seminar room was thankfully in one of the newer buildings at the university so he had his phone plugged in charging next to him. The perks of the modern world, and the bright white walls of the seminar room were covered in all sorts of posters, decorative things and lights that really help to make the place feel modern and interesting.

Tom took a large sip of the sweet, creamy, slightly too bitter coffee and enjoyed its sharp aftertaste and the strong coffee aroma that filled his senses. He didn't need coffee like so many other university students did, he just liked the taste.

It would have liked it more if this cup wasn't so bitter but he didn't care. He was in a room filled with other queer students and that's all that mattered to him.

The long horseshoe ring of white tables were filled with other university students as they came in. Tom was glad to see some friends and some new faces.

He had never seen a small group of female students in the far corner before. They were talking about everything they possibly could it seemed, and Tom wanted to try to tell them apart but they all looked the same.

Their jeans, black hoodies and longish shoulder-length hair made it impossible for him to tell them apart.

He was so glad when his friend Beth came to sit next to him. She was always so positive, smiling and she looked great in her grey dress that normally wouldn't work on anyone but on Beth it was always going to work.

The floor-to-ceiling windows opposite Tom took up two entire walls of the room and Tom had to force himself not to people watch too much. But he couldn't deny the argument outside between a young woman in a black trench coat and her boyfriend in a black hoody was fascinating to watch.

Whatever the man had done wrong, his girlfriend

was furious.

"Hey Tom," Beth said.

"Hi, how's the girlfriend?" Tom asked, knowing Beth was pansexual and really did love her girlfriend.

"Yeah she's good thanks. But I don't want to sound stupid but what actually is a zine?" Beth asked trying to keep her voice down.

"I am so glad you said that," Tom said, "I have no idea either. I just signed up for the work op because it was gay-related,"

"Fair enough, how are the parents and home life?" Beth asked.

Tom shrugged. "Dad just denies I'm gay and mother just being mother about it,"

"You should take a photo of you being here and post it," Beth said. "You never know it might be exactly what your family needs to realise you are gay,"

Tom shook his head. As much as he would love posting anything gay-related on social media so his parents could see it, he didn't want to cause that much trouble. He was still being gay and exploring himself and what being gay meant to him, but he wasn't going to be rash about it.

A moment later Tom noticed a large woman with bright orange hair and a dress that made her look like she was from the 90s child TV industry came into the room with a man behind her. They looked to be in charge and Tom got the sense that he was going to like them.

"Hi everyone, I'm Jess," the woman said, "and

relax we know you've never heard of a zine before. But we're talk about it tonight, but just think about it as a little booklet that's stuck together,"

Tom looked at Beth. "Well that's it then all our problems are solved. We're experts now,"

Beth playfully hit him on the arm and they both laughed, but Tom was sure they worked for the university if they were going to keep giving answers to questions that were clear as mud.

The door opened again.

"Sorry I'm late," a man said with a slightly high-pitched voice.

Tom just looked as he looked at the man. He was fucking amazing as he came through the door. Tom's heart pounded. His head went light. His mouth stopped working.

He had no idea who the hell this beautiful man was but he was to die for. Tom seriously liked his fit, sexy body that was tight and he didn't look to have a single gram of body fat on that divine body of his.

Tom couldn't help but focus on the man's beautiful shortish blond hair that was styled over and parted to the left. He was so beautiful, sexy and Tom really couldn't get over how fit this man was.

And Tom knew it was a strange thing to get turned-on by but he was really pleased that the man had perfectly smooth, sexy arms without a single hair on them. He was the definition of a beautiful twink.

Tom just grinned at the hot man until he realised the only seat left in the entire horseshoe was right next to him on the left.

And the beautiful twink was walking straight towards him, making Tom a lot happier than he ever wanted to admit even to himself.

CHAPTER 4
15th March 2023
Canterbury, England

Henry flat out knew that he seriously needed to stop obsessing so much about his appearance before he went out in public. He shouldn't have spent so much making sure that his hair was styled right, his clothes were okay and that he *felt* okay in his own skin.

Henry just hated how after so many years of not being comfortable in a body that really didn't belong to him, he still felt a little uncomfortable. But he wasn't sure if he was actually uncomfortable or if he just didn't know how to feel comfortable.

After spending at extra hour making sure he was happy and he felt as manly as he could get for now, he was annoyed with himself he was slightly late for the Zine workshop. He went inside, said hello to everyone and just noticed someone brand-new.

An extremely hot brand-new man.

Henry just stared in the doorway of the seminar room at the utterly sexy man that was sitting next to the only spare seat in the entire room.

His heart pounded. His stomach churned. His hands shook as he realised he was about to sit next to a guy he was really attracted too. Something he hadn't done for ages.

Henry admired the gorgeous man's short curly black hair, fit, slim body that didn't make him look like a rake but didn't make him seem average by any definition. His piercing emerald green eyes were sharp, focused and beautiful.

Henry really liked how the man's emerald eyes felt like they were searching for him and making Henry believe, even for a moment, that he was a beautiful man and maybe he could have a great future in the body he was meant to have.

Then Henry realised he was standing in the same place for a few seconds too long so he forced himself to move towards the beautiful man, and for a moment his legs didn't want to move.

He forced himself to move and then he went over to the sexy man that was still focusing on him.

A tiny amount of fear, concern and nervousness washed over Henry, because now he was trapped sitting next to a wonderfully beautiful man for the next few hours. It wasn't a bad thing, but what if the beautiful man stopped liking him if the conversation turned towards trans people?

Henry shook the idea away. He just couldn't tell

the beautiful man for now, especially after all the negative stuff he had read online and Henry knew that he needed to accept himself first before he would ever get into a serious relationship.

That was simply how the world worked.

"So everyone," Jess said a moment before Henry could introduce himself to the beautiful man next to him. "Let's talk about zines,"

Henry had to admit over the next ten minutes of the very passionate presentation, he was gripped by the man's and woman's energy and passion for zines. And they were a lot cooler than Henry realised because they were little booklets that anyone could stick together and design around a certain topic.

Jess had passed around a ton of zines and some were very sweet and U-rated but others were very, very hot filled with even hotter naked men.

"I wouldn't mind making a zine like these ones," the hot man said flicking through some exotic male photos in one zine.

Henry smiled. He couldn't agree more, but he had a feeling that the university would hardly let them make a zine like those.

"So," the man, Jim, said, "Outreach have asked us to help you create a Mythbusting Zine. You might want to talk about your own experiences, queer myths you've heard and anything that you might have wanted to hear as a child,"

Henry grinned. He had no idea at all where he would start with his pages that would go into the

Outreach. He would have loved to learn as a child as feeling uncomfortable in your biological body was okay to feel. He really would have loved to know where he could have spoken about these feelings and he would have liked even more to know that there was a community that would accept him for who he truly was.

Those were exactly the sort of things he would have liked to have known.

After a few more moments of instructions and handing out paper, scissors and coloured pens, Henry looked at the beautiful man and smiled.

"I'm Henry," he said really glad that his real name came off his tongue so much easier now than it had last year. There wasn't any hesitation.

"I'm Tom," the hot man said picking up a pack of purple pens. "What do you think you'll start your pages with? Experiences, myths, anything else?"

Henry frowned a little but forced himself to smile. He was only going to do trans myths and facts because he simply needed that as a child and he never ever wanted another child to go through the adolescence he did, Henry just didn't want to tell Tom that this soon.

"I'm really not sure," Henry said hating lying to Tom. "What about you?"

Henry watched as Tom's beautifully smooth hands picked up a pad of red and orange and blue paper and started writing down a whole bunch of myths he had heard.

Henry laughed at some of them. They were brilliant myths about being gay was a choice, how everything in the world was rigged against straight people and more.

"Just some stuff my parents say at times," Tom said, "so I'm going to argue with them on paper and in a Zine,"

"Ask for a copy and give it to them," Henry said smiling.

Tom laughed. "That would go down like a lead balloon but it would be funny to watch. It was bad enough watching their reactions to the fact I'm gay,"

"My parents had the same reaction to me being trans," Henry said.

As soon as the words left his mouth Henry instantly regretted it and he wanted to check his appearance, to run away and just get out of here as soon as he could.

It would have killed him if someone as beautiful as Tom would reject him for being trans.

Thankfully Tom just grinned in a wonderful schoolboy sort of way.

ACCEPTING LOVE

CHAPTER 5
15th March 2023
Canterbury, England

"Okay,"

Tom really didn't have anything else to say to Henry as he told him he was trans. Granted because his parents had kept him so divorced from the queer community, Tom wasn't a 100% sure what that meant in terms of he wasn't sure if Henry was a biological man that wanted to become a woman or vice versa.

But he could see how beautiful Henry was with his sharp pointy face, wonderful longish blond hair and his perfectly smooth skin. Tom really couldn't have cared less at that moment if Henry was a man, woman or whatever. He was beautiful and that was all that mattered.

Tom had to force himself not to stroke Henry's perfectly smooth cheek, run his fingers through Henry's delightfully short hair and it shook every single gram of Tom's willpower not to stare at

Henry's soft, full lips.

Henry was perfect in every way.

"Tom," Beth said.

Tom rolled his eyes as he only really wanted to talk to Henry but clearly his friend had other ideas.

"One moment," Tom said feeling guilty for looking away from Henry even for a short time.

Tom looked at Beth who was doing some incredible drawings of her flatmates and how they joked about not letting her into the kitchen because she's attracted to pans. Beth had a great sense of humour and Tom couldn't help himself but smile.

Then three of their other friends were also sitting there talking, drawing and gossiping about the Mythbusting programme and a whole bunch of other stuff.

"Yeah," Tom said. "What do you need?"

"Do you have a red pen over there please?" Bath asked. "And definitely ask him out. You're clearly into him,"

"I know I am," he said to Beth passing her a red pen and shaking his head because his friend wasn't giving him any time to talk to Henry before interfering, saying that they needed to date.

Tom looked back at Henry and smiled because he was drawing something. It might have been a cat, a dog or maybe a donkey. He could tell Henry didn't do any art degrees that was for sure, but his hand movements were artful, careful and deliberate and it was just kind of nice watching him work.

"What are you starting with?" Tom asked.

"The basics. Starting off with how people think being trans is a choice," Henry said.

Tom nodded and he really hoped that his next question wouldn't be worded too badly. "I know it isn't a choice, but what, but does it feel like? If you don't mind me asking of course,"

"It feels you like don't belong in your own body," Henry said liking how carefully Tom was wording it. "You know how in school there are always boy and girl groups. You sort of just know what group you belong in, don't you?"

Tom nodded wanting to learn as much as he could.

"Like you feel at home in the boy group but when I was sitting with the girls at school. I hated it. I was different to them, I didn't have anything in common and I kept wanting to sit in the boy group,"

Tom nodded. At least he understood that Henry was a biological female that was now a very beautiful man, and Tom knew it shouldn't have mattered if Henry was a man or woman but he was still sorting through what his own parents had told him over the years.

And it wasn't like you come turn on the news some days and not find at least one anti-trans story in the media. Tom really liked that he was finally starting to learn the truth behind what being trans was actually all about.

"What else can you tell me?" Tom asked

knowing he was asking his questions too carefully.

Henry stopped and looked at him. Tom was surprised that Henry didn't seem sure if he was joking or not. Maybe no one had ever asked Henry these sort of questions before and Tom had no idea the impact that these questions might have on someone.

Tom knew from his own experience that when someone was asking gay questions, he was still a little defensive, but that spoke more about his past than anything else.

"I don't know where to start," Henry said.

"I really like your hair," Tom said, "and you honestly look amazing,"

Henry just grinned and Tom had to admit it was the most beautiful smile he had ever seen and he seriously hoped he would keep seeing that smile again and again because it was so perfect. Just like Henry.

CHAPTER 6
15th March 2023
Canterbury, England

After three wonderful hours, Henry was feeling so damn happy as he went along the long concrete path with thick silver birch trees lining it, as he went towards his university accommodation. It was great that Tom had wanted to walk him home even though his own flat was on the other side of campus.

But Henry really, really liked the company.

The night was warm and Henry enjoyed having Tom so close to him as they were the only two on the long path. Every so often the talking, shouting and drunken singing of other students stopped the silence but Henry didn't mind.

The air was sweet, a little damp and Henry knew that the shared house filled with Caribbean students were probably cooking one of their great dishes from home again. They did host legendary parties too and Henry really did like the taste of their cooking.

Henry looked down at Tom's hand. It was just loosely hanging down by his side and Henry really wanted to touch it, hold it and just enjoy having a moment with Tom.

The entire evening had been great, filled with laughs, great stories about people's experiences of being queer (both the positive and the negative) and Henry was relieved that he felt part of a community.

That was definitely one of the problems about looking up things online about being trans. There were a lot of fake articles and more saying how lesbians, gays and bisexuals just didn't want anything to do with trans people.

Thankfully Henry hadn't experienced that tonight and he doubted it would be. So it was fun and nice and relaxing just being himself tonight with Tom and the others.

And the best thing was that no one cared about who he had been and who he was now. Henry still wasn't sure that the realisation of what had meant for him had hit him yet but it was still a great feeling to have.

Yet it wasn't quite as great as Tom, sweet precious Tom telling him that he looked beautiful, and that he was a beautiful man.

Even now, Henry had to fight back tears, calm down his stomach filled with butterflies and the urge just hug Tom. It was the only first ever that someone Henry really cared about or was attracted to had confirmed that he was a man.

He wasn't sure if he was going to try and explain the feeling to Adam or any of his other friends later on, but it meant the world to Henry. No one had ever confirmed his real gender before to him and now he understood why other people had said it made them feel so great.

After a few more moments of going down the path, Henry looked at his big semi-detached house that wasn't much to look at, but he felt sad, hopeless and much of the high he had just had was now gone.

He was going to have to leave Tom.

Henry took Tom's hand and his. Henry loved the sheer power and feeling of attraction, intense chemistry that flowed between them.

Henry so badly wanted to kiss Tom, feel his body against him and maybe even do something-

Henry shook the thought away. No, he never wanted to do something adult because he hated his lower body so much and he had never accepted it. Something he needed to work on but Henry had no idea how.

"What's wrong?" Tom said biting his lower lip and gently stroking Henry's hand.

Henry loved how gently and lovingly Tom was touching him and all he wanted to do was kiss him, but he forced himself to behave. He couldn't get involved with anyone too heavily for now, not until he fully accepted himself and that would just take time.

"Nothing," Henry said hating that he was lying to

Tom. "I think I'm just tired or something and need to go to bed or something,"

"Yeah I get them. I've had a long day too," Tom said knowing that Henry was lying, "but I've enjoyed meeting you and knowing you. Is there any chance that we could meet-up again?"

Henry grinned. "We could go out for dinner on Friday if you want?"

"A date?" Tom said rubbing Henry's hands even more.

Henry laughed. "Yes a date then or just two people having dinner together and talking about life, gay stuff and everything else that pops up."

"No," Tom said. "Not two people together, two men together,"

Henry felt a wave of intense emotion wash over him as he loved how firmly, supportively and caringly Tom had said those words that he had always wanted to hear.

"See you Friday beautiful," Tom said as he walked away.

Henry just stood there in the darkness because he couldn't believe how great tonight had been and he was really looking forward to knowing how things were going to get even better on Friday.

CHAPTER 7
17ᵗʰ March 2023
Gillingham, England

Over the past two days of texting, calling and just getting to know beautiful Henry, Tom was really surprised how chatty he actually was. He had to admit that when he first met Henry and even after the great walk just the two of them down that long concrete path after the Zine session, Tom had no idea henry liked talking so much until he started messaging him.

Tom didn't have a problem at all with it, because he loved, really, really loved just talking and getting to know the amazing man he was starting to like more and more. Granted Henry had a weird way of just throwing random topics into their conversations no matter if it was relevant or not. Like how they were both pro-monarchy, thought billionaires should be made to pay more tax and how transphobia just wasn't okay.

It was great.

But Tom had never ever expected to travel a good hour on the very reliable (not) trains from Canterbury in south Kent to Medway in North Kent for their date. Tom had no idea why Henry wanted to come here for their date but he didn't really care.

The point was that he got to spend it with Henry and that seriously was all that mattered.

Tom allowed beautiful Henry in his tight black jeans, black t-shirt that highlighted just how fit his body was and white trainers led him into the pizza restaurant that Henry used to go to a lot as a child.

Tom really liked how it was large with black shiny tiling covered two parrel walls before an even larger floor-to-ceiling window covered the wall facing the car park. The car park itself was massive and filled with tons of black, white and blue cars of so many different types that Tom really wasn't sure he could name any of them.

He was useless when it came to cars.

As a cute young waiter in the black and red uniform of the restaurant took them towards their table, Tom had to force himself not to stare at Henry's great-looking ass as he went first.

Tom made himself look at the five other rows of black and red booths that provided a lot of privacy from other tables, and it was great that the booths still allowed them to look at the car park and see who else was walking about outside.

Tom didn't know why he liked that little feature but in case Henry needed to leave the table for anything important, at least he could people watch or something.

"Here's your table," the waiter said and Tom smiled at him as the waiter's face suggested that he already suspected this was a date already.

Tom didn't know if it was embarrassing or not that it was clear as day they were on a date.

He took a seat in the really supportive, soft and comfortable red and black booth that was normally reserved for families of four and it was nice. Henry was just flat out beautiful as he sat down and scanned the QR code on the table so they could order.

Tom couldn't help himself but stare and admire how stunning Henry was tonight. He didn't doubt for a moment Henry had been scared about his appearance, making sure that he passed but Tom didn't care.

Henry had the most beautiful blond hair ever that was parted so perfectly to the left that Tom really wanted to run his fingers through it. And Henry's soft, smooth skin reflected the bright yellow lights of the restaurant perfectly.

He was just so beautiful, wonderful and perfect.

"So how does this restaurant work again?" Tom asked clocking that there were no wait staff walking around so he presumed that no one was going to take their order.

"We order it all on the app that I have up now," Henry said studying the app intensely.

Tom picked up a menu on the edge of the booth

and started reading it. There were so many incredible types and flavours and combinations of pizza that Tom didn't know where to start.

The BBQ chicken combo sounded great and he did love the rich, smoky flavour of BBQ sauce. And there were tons of different crust options that he was really looking forward to exploring.

He would have whatever Henry wanted but he was really hoping for stuffed crust because you really couldn't beat it.

"Did you want to get a sharing one?" Henry asked.

Tom was surprised and he froze a little. He had never ever gotten a sharing thing on a date before, and it sounded stupid but wouldn't a sharing thing make it clear to everyone that they were on a date. And what if they judged Henry for being trans and-

It wasn't like there were actually many people in the restaurant anyway because it was slightly before the dinner crowd came in.

So Tom shook the thought away. He knew he was being silly and overreacting to something that was perfectly innocent, and that was one of the reasons why he wanted to date beautiful Henry in the first place. He wanted to experience being gay and he just wanted to know that going on dates were perfectly okay.

And as Tom looked at Henry with that wonderful hair, face and smile, Tom was really pleased with how right, natural and amazing this felt.

"Yes please," Tom said knowing he was really looking forward to getting a sharing pizza. "Let's have stuffed crust and BBQ,"

Henry grinned. "Maybe this dating stuff can work out. You're a man after my own heart,"

"And you're definitely a man after mine," Tom said knowing the words might have sounded a little clumsy but he had really gotten the sense over the past two days that Henry really liked it when Tom confirmed his real gender with him.

"Why are you so nice to me about gender stuff?" Henry asked really liking how Tom confirmed his gender in subtle ways. "I mean I really like it, but no one has ever done it for me before,"

Tom shrugged. "I don't know. I like you and that's probably why. But don't your friends and family, or at least parents confirm your gender,"

Tom was a little surprised when Henry's face fell and then looked like he forced himself to smile again, but it definitely didn't reach his wonderful eyes.

"Not always. My friends are great but I've definitely lost some friends, especially female friends because they said I've given up on female hood, whatever that means, and my parents. They always wanted a daughter so now they're trying but they want me to be a daughter,"

Tom felt a wave of anger wash over him. It was so disgusting that his parents didn't like him for being him, but then Tom forced himself to take a long deep breath because he was only getting angry because of his own parents.

"Well I'm glad you're a man," Tom said and as the waiter came over to give them their glasses for their refillable Diet Cokes, Tom didn't even look at the waiter.

All he cared about was the stunning man sitting across from him. A man he was seriously starting to fall for.

CHAPTER 8
17ᵗʰ March 2023
Gillingham, England

Henry had absolutely no idea that all he had really, really wanted out of the date was to just talk about everything and nothing with a great man that accepted him for who he was.

After two great hours of talking, eating and just going from one topic of conversation to another without a single moment of silence, Henry was convinced that Tom wasn't real. Because surely a man like Tom that listened, supported him and wanted to talk about everything that came to mind just couldn't be real?

Henry picked at the very last slice of BBQ pizza on his plate and he still couldn't believe how sensational it had been. The smoky, tangy, acidity from the BBQ had been perfectly paired with the flavourful roasted chicken that caused an explosion of flavour to form on his tongue.

But the best part of the pizza just had to be the cheesy, garlicy, buttery stuffed crust. It was incredible and it was even better than the dishes he used to have with his parents and siblings when he came here as a child.

It was such a brilliant meal and an even better date.

"How often did you used to come here with your family?" Tom asked finishing off his slice of pizza.

"I don't know," Henry said really not knowing. "My family normally comes from Medway but when I started university in Canterbury we all moved down there. I actually applied to university down there because my parents were starting new jobs there anyway,"

Tom nodded and Henry loved it how he looked like he was hanging onto every word. Henry had no idea if Tom did this in lectures but if he did, he would have been shocked if Tom wasn't top of the class.

"So we would come here maybe once a month as a treat. Well that was if me and my sister and brother were behaving," Henry said grinning. He really did miss his family at times.

"Where you three hellraisers?"

Henry laughed. "You could say that. Let's just say that I wasn't a very easy to live with child when I was a teenager. Part of it, as you can expect, me hating being a woman and feeling so uncomfortable in my own skin that I took it out on people and things,"

Henry just stopped as he realised how pathetic, weird and awful that made him sound but Tom was just amazing as he always was. Henry didn't doubt Tom was judging him inside but he had the decency not to show it.

"I couldn't imagine what it was like," Tom said wanting Henry to know he wasn't judging him. "And I know from being gay with bad parents it can be hard,"

Henry wanted to hug him so much but he forced himself to go on.

"And then I was just a normal teenager too. I was annoyed at the world, angry at my parents and I did all the normal teenager stuff too," Henry said. "Got any teen rebellion stories?"

Tom grinned. "When I was 16, I knew I was gay and my parents were moaning about gays one night and I wasn't out yet, so the next day we went to a massive department store and my parents were checking out a display of really nice clothes,"

Henry nodded. He liked where this was heading.

"And my mother was looking at a white shirt that they normally would have called *too manly* and my dad was looking at another shirt that was *too girly*. So I pushed over the display, it all came crashing down and I was banned from the store,"

"Oh," Henry said. "That's a story and a half. What did your parents say?"

"I don't know. My parents never spoke about and they got a whole bunch of clothing, probably so the store didn't press charges,"

Henry laughed. "At least they have some kind of protective instinct,"

"I mean they aren't bad parents actually. They just don't know how to handle the fact I'm gay, liked men and they don't like the fact that the path they determined for me isn't going to happen,"

Henry had no idea what he meant by a predetermined path. Surely that was bad parenting or something and a parent should always allow their children to do whatever they wanted in life. Henry gestured him to continue.

"Oh they wanted me to marry the girl next door, have a ton of kids and just be a straight man with a straight wedding and everything else,"

Henry took a large sip of his drink and enjoyed how great, calming and natural this felt.

"How many clothes do you have?" Tom asked.

Henry just looked at him, he had no idea what sort of question that was.

"I mean, all the summer stuff is starting to come into the shops. Do you have male summer clothes?" Tom asked.

Henry slowly shook his head. He had only really started dressing properly last winter and he hadn't had a chance yet to go proper shopping, mainly because he didn't feel confident enough until now.

And even then it was a stretch to say he was confident.

"Would you come with me?" Henry asked.

"It can be our next date," Tom said grinning.

Henry shook his head. "Wouldn't that be a bad date or something? Do you really want to go clothes shopping as a real date?"

"Normally, definitely not. There isn't anything worse I can think of, but I do need some summer stuff, it's what you need and I love spending time with you,"

Henry smiled because he was really, really starting to wonder if there was a single thing wrong with Henry.

He was perfect in so many ways and Henry just couldn't stop wondering how badly it was going to hurt when it all went wrong.

Because surely it would, wouldn't it?

CHAPTER 9
19th March 2023
Canterbury, England

Out of everything Tom had ever wanted to do for a guy, and a really beautiful one at that, he had never ever wanted to go clothes shopping with one before. He just didn't like shopping at all and normally he preferred to buy things online, get surprised when the sizes were actually true and then enjoy the clothes when he got stuff that fitted him.

The joys of online shopping.

As Tom led Henry into a great little clothing shop just off the cobblestoned high street of Canterbury, Tom was pleased the layout of the store was exactly like he remembered it. All the female racks, drawers and models were on the left-hand side of the store and the men's were on the right.

It was great that the clothing store still had the bright white walls covered in fit as fuck pictures of male underwear models, that were hot but they were nothing compared to Henry.

There were a lot of racks filled with shorts, shirts and thin summer trousers with all sorts of colours and textures. Tom had to admit some of them looked faulty but this was one of the cheapest and best quality stores to get clothes from on a student's budget so he was willing to spend some time in here.

And it meant he got to see Henry's beautiful face so that was always a great incentive.

Tom really wanted to hold Henry's hand tight because it just felt the right and natural thing to do on a date like this, but he had tried earlier and Henry had subtly let go.

Tom didn't mind too much, because he knew this was all new for Henry, so as much as he wanted to hold his hand, kiss him and run his fingers through his hair, Tom was forcing himself to be patient no matter how hard that was getting.

"Let's get you some shorts," Tom said leading Henry carefully by the hand over to a large display of different shorts in blacks, blues and greens.

Tom picked up a Denim pair in black, he really wasn't fussed by clothes but these looked good. He went over to a mirror and placed them over his jeans and he could see how these might look good on him when the summer truly came.

He looked over at Henry smiling but Henry looked like he was a deer in headlights.

Tom went over to him and made sure no one was looking at them. He knew there was a security camera right above them but he didn't want to point it out to Henry.

"What do you need today?" Tom asked. "Let's start off small,"

Henry nodded and Tom gently took his hand and placed it on the black Denim shorts. Henry didn't seem too interested in the black shorts but Tom was glad when he started looking through a bunch of green shorts.

They certainly weren't a colour that Tom would have gone for but he was sure that Henry could make everything look beautiful.

Then Henry picked them up and ran his fingers through the fabric and placed them over his own blue jeans. He looked at Tom.

Tom smiled. "They look good. Why don't you come over here and see what you look like? Or go into the changing rooms,"

Tom knew he was pushing his luck here but pushing Henry out of his comfort zone might have been a good point.

"No," Henry said quietly,

Tom went so close to Henry that he felt Henry's wonderful body heat against him. "I'm here for you. Nothing bad's going to happen and you are a man. It's normal for you and every other man to look at themselves in the mirror buying clothes,"

Henry nodded and Tom watched him as he went over to the mirror next to the display and looked at himself with the green shorts in his hands.

Tom was tempted to say how beautiful he looked but Henry looked lost in the moment and he looked so stunning as he smiled at the clothes he was buying.

Tom had no idea what it was like for him buying summer clothes for the first time, and these summer clothes reflected who he actually was. And part of Tom didn't want to know he was beautiful, perfect and so sexy that Tom didn't care about anything else.

"Where are the, you know um, changing rooms in here?" Henry asked failing to hide how nervous he was.

"I'll take you," Tom said, "did you want to take any other clothes in there?"

Henry shook his head.

"Okay that's fine," Tom said wanting to be as supportive as possible. "Baby steps. Let's just do baby steps,"

Henry looked and Tom led him over to the back of the store where the changing rooms were and he nodded to the middle-aged woman behind the till that was giving them a very supportive smile.

Something Tom was really glad Henry didn't see.

But just before the red curtain of the changing cubicle shut, Tom smiled at the beautiful man he was falling for.

"I'm proud of you, you know?" he said and he meant every single word of it.

CHAPTER 10
19th March 2023
Canterbury, England

Later that night Henry sat on top of a very high bar stool next to the large black kitchen island that him and his housemates shared in their surprisingly clean kitchen. It had been ages since the others had decided to clean it but the kitchen looked great with its shiny silver worktops, perfectly shiny floors and even the kitchen island that served as their dining table wasn't sticky at all.

Henry wasn't sure what had happened earlier but there had to have been a party or an accident or something to make the others decide to clean for the first time in ages.

Henry smiled as Adam, Jane and Jordan all lowered their large mugs of coffee as they sat down. Henry couldn't believe how badly his friends had wanted to talk to him about the past few days and Henry was really pleased that they just wanted to know that he was okay.

It was even better that Jane had baked two gluten-free pizzas for all of them with great toppings like tomatoes, Spanish ham and a whole lot of cheese from the Continent that Henry really hadn't known existed before now.

Henry had wanted to wear some of the new clothes he had bought earlier but everything felt so rushed. In the space of four days he had gone from not knowing anything about his real gender identity and how that functioned in the real world to having a great man that confirmed him, wanted to support him and Henry didn't doubt if things kept going as they did that Tom would love him in the end.

It was all too much so Henry told his friends all this.

"Mate," Jordan said, "I don't want to discredit you but you do realise this is everything you've ever wanted?"

Henry shook his head. "I wanted to accept myself first before I got a boyfriend that did it all for me? And come on this is happening too fast, isn't it?"

Jane smiled. "Honey, what is actually happening too fast? All you have done in four days is have a dinner date and go clothing shopping,"

"Something Jane has said she would do with you for ages," Adam said.

"No," Jane said, "I wasn't thinking about what shopping might actually mean to *him* though. Shopping with a girl for guy clothes is different than shopping with a guy for guy clothes,"

Henry smiled at her. All of his friends were flat out amazing but maybe they were right, maybe he was overreacting because he never expected things to go this right, this perfect and this wonderfully so soon.

Jordan took a massive sip of coffee. "Can I ask a home life question please?"

"Um sure," Henry said looking at Jane and Adam for support. Something that both subtly nodded immediately.

"Mate, I know you've mentioned before that you knew you were a man when you were 13, 14. But why did it take you so long to start transition even socially?" Jordan asked.

Henry supposed it was a fair question because he hadn't really spoken about it much anyway to anyone.

"Because my parents and family don't like transpeople so childhood was a scary time and place. And I actually never planned to tell that that I was trans until… until I couldn't keep it a secret anymore," Henry said.

"So until you came back with a beard?" Jane asked.

Henry laughed. "Yeah exactly. I only told my parents because I was at a doctor's appointment and the woman wanted to know a ton about my family's medical history,"

"Why?" Adam asked. "How does what runs in your parent's families impact hormone therapy and whatnot?"

Henry smiled as Adam's voice went from really confident at the start to completely unsure about what he was talking about by the end of the question. But Henry didn't blame him, it was only in the past year when he realised he just wanted to fuck his parents and he needed to transition for himself that he had stated properly researching it.

"I don't know. I stopped listening as soon as I realised my parents were going to find out today that I was trans and starting a procedure they flat out hated,"

"Then mate," Jordan said, "what happened when you told home?"

Henry lifted up his coffee mug to use as a sort of barrier between him and Jordan. "Nothing. Nothing happened at all and it was tense as hell for a few weeks but they don't care about me being trans, they're trying but failing and honestly, I don't mention it,"

"If it works it works," Jordan said carefully.

Henry shrugged. It was a shame that it did work like that because he would have loved to tell his parents about what was happening and he would have liked to have their input and opinions on matters. But he knew they were never ever going to be respectful enough to even start listening to him.

"When was the last time you called them?" Adam asked.

"Since January," Henry said.

"Then maybe call them. Maybe they miss you so

much that they're more open to talk about stuff. I remember your mother always banging on about wanting you to buy more good clothes?"

Henry bit his lower lip because that was true. His mother would be proud that he bought good, stylish clothes for a change. Even though he only bought cheap awful woman's clothes because he knew at some point he would get so angry with having to wear the damn things he would destroy them.

"Maybe I'll call her," Henry said taking out his phone and then he realised his friends actually wanted to watch.

Henry dialled a video call but his mother denied it and instead did a voice-only call. It was a little weird but his mother was technophobic as hell.

"Hi Hen," his youngest nephew said, someone he hadn't been 'allowed' to see in months since his sister had found out he was trans.

Henry almost choked on the coffee he was drinking.

"Hi buddy, how's school?" Henry asked.

"Fun. I got to learn about dinos, big, big, scary dinos today. They're cool," his nephew said.

"They sure are buddy," Henry said.

"Nanny!" his nephew shouted as Henry heard the phone change hands. "I wanna talk to Uncle Henry!"

Henry forced himself not to cry as his little precious nephew was probably the only member of his family that called him Henry every single time without question.

"Hi Harriet," his mother said naturally.

Henry sighed. "You got to stop doing that mum,"

He heard his mother sigh on the other side of the phone. "I'm sorry, I really am Hen. I'm trying but your sister's round and little nephew. You can come round if you want,"

Henry really, really wanted to but he knew that it wouldn't be as easy as that.

"You know Sophie wouldn't let me round but you would say I would come round and everyone would be magically gone in the twenty minutes it would take me to get *home*,"

"Don't take that tone with me," his mother said, "but you know your sister doesn't want you to talk to Daniel. Can't you respect her? Can't you respect any of us?"

Henry laughed and liked it that Jane was hugging him.

"Respect you guys? Mother the first thing you said when you pick up the phone is Deadname me. That isn't cool and I did call you for a reason,"

"What?" his mother asked, not sounding that interested.

"I tried shopping today and I finally got my good clothes like you always wanted me too," Henry said smiling because the clothes were great.

"Woman's clothes?" his mother asked hopeful.

"Mother, this needs to stop. You either need to

start showing support for me being a man or you can only call me when you're feeling nice,"

His mother laughed. "Just remember who pays for your accommodation Harriet. And I can stop it anytime I want then where will you live next term? Because you aren't living here,"

Henry cut the line and threw his phone across the kitchen.

He hated his parents, his family and everything else about his life.

CHAPTER 11
19th March 2023
Canterbury, England

Tom was really glad that he had decided to give Henry some space because of how overwhelming and brand-new today was for him. And Tom was rather impressed with himself for not kissing Henry as they parted ways outside Henry's university shared house because Tom so badly wanted to kiss him.

There wasn't anything more that he wanted.

Tom leant against the comfortable fabric of the black sofa in his shared kitchenette. He had just finished a great run at the gym, lifted some weights and he had come back for some dinner before he showered.

He was really surprised that Jasmine had invited about three of their mutual friends over from his psychology course, so Tom might have been a little sweaty but it was still great to see them.

Even Beth was there.

Tom nodded his thanks to Jasmine as she passed him and Beth on the sofa a piping hot bowl of curry to each other. Whilst Jessica, Steve and Anna sat on the bar stools around the kitchen island.

Tom hissed as he placed the bowl of curry on his lap because it was way too hot to even remotely enjoy for now.

"What's everyone up to?" Tom asked.

"Seriously?" Jessica asked. "Have you forgotten about that massive essay on persuasion that's due in in two weeks?"

"No," Tom said smiling. "I just don't hang about and I do essays and coursework assignments faster so I can relax for the rest of the term,"

"Fair enough," Jessica said. "That was sort of my plan earlier in the term but last month I started volunteering at that refugee centre in Dover,"

"Oh cool," Beth said.

Tom couldn't agree more. "How's that going?"

"Well," Jessica said rolling her eyes, "it's a nightmare because all these people are real refugees that are fleeing horrific crimes and yet the government wants to send them all back into the jaws of people they're fleeing,"

"Disgusting," Tom said.

"Definitely," Anna said. "I've just been working on assignments and stuff. I sometimes do that Reading Outreach opportunities but that's it these days,"

Tom smiled because everyone knew that Anna

had a very passionate and loving relationship with her boyfriend, but he couldn't understand why Anna wanted to hide it.

"What about you then Steve?" Jasmine asked sounding like she knew exactly what he was going to say.

Steve laughed. "I've met someone."

Tom looked at Steve and he had a feeling that he knew who it was.

"Are you finally dating that woman you always sit next to in Stats class?" Tom asked. "After saying you would never ever date her, and you would rather die than have to sit next to her and watch her eating?"

"Well yeah," Steve said. "I still can't watch her eat but we are together and loving it."

"We're gonna have to meet her," Tom said, "at some point,"

"When are we meeting your boyfriend?" Jasmine asked.

Tom froze. He hadn't really told many people about his new relationship with Henry, because he had wanted to see how it went and he'd been so busy with his charity work, gym and running that he hadn't had time to see his friends too much.

"What's his name?" Steve asked.

"Don't you mean *her* name?" Jasmine asked making it sound like a joke.

Tom just looked at her and he felt Beth get really angry next to him.

"That is not okay to say," Tom said trying to

keep his voice very level. "He is a man and that's okay. If you have a problem with that then go away. Now,"

Anna and Steve looked at each other. "Is he trans?"

Tom forced himself not to look at them too angrily but he had no idea why they were making it sound like it was a problem or weird or something that wasn't right.

"Yes he is," Tom said noticing how he was failing to keep his voice level.

"Oh," Anna said. "That's… different,"

Tom looked at her. "What do you mean? He isn't strange, weird or anything and he is a wonderful guy,"

Anna smiled. "I know, I don't doubt that. It's just you hear a lot of stories and I've never met a trans person before,"

"Of course you haven't met a trans person before," Tom said, "because they are a minority of a minority but that doesn't mean that the stories and rubbish you see on the news is real,"

Tom tried to take long deep breaths to calm himself down but he just couldn't. His friends really did sound like they were struggling to understand that he was dating a trans man. A very beautiful man at that.

"I know Henry," Beth said, "and he is a great guy and he'll be a great boyfriend to Tom,"

Tom just shook his head as all his friends looked at each other like they didn't know whether Beth could be believed or not.

Tom stood up. "This is ridiculous. I have supported all of your relationships without question even when I knew they were going to end in a clusterfuck. And the one time I'm in a relationship with a hot guy that I really, really like you guys can't support me,"

"He isn't a guy," Steve and Jasmine said.

"Fuck you," Tom said walking off.

And Tom knew he never ever wanted to see Steve and Jasmine ever again. A minor problem as they were best friends and Jasmine shared a kitchen with him.

Tom was not impressed. He was angry.

ACCEPTING LOVE

CHAPTER 12
19th March 2023
Canterbury, England

Henry was so glad that his friends were sitting around the large kitchen island with him because he had no idea how he felt about himself, the future and anything to do with his family. He hated his family but he never ever wanted to lose them. Especially not precious little Daniel.

Henry just let Jane hug him a little longer as they all spoke about other university topics that didn't relate to accommodation or family at all, and Henry really did love his friends for it.

Jordan and Adam were talking about sports, because apparently that would help Henry feel better. It sort of did but it was cute when Jordan tried to ask him what he thought about a football technique and Henry didn't know football. He didn't even know the sport had any techniques.

Surely it was all just kicking a ball about.

"Thank you guys," Henry said, gently pushing Jane away from him and he picked up his new mug of coffee that Adam had made him earlier.

"You know," Jane said, "if your bitch of a mother doesn't want to see your clothes, I'm willing? And I know Adam could use some fashion ideas,"

"No woman," Adam said, "I don't need any more clothes. I said when we go to Greece in July I can wear all my clothes from last year,"

"Yes," Jane said, "and that would be great if those clothes actually were bought last year. You've had those shorts and shirts ever since you were 15 and the colour's bleached out of them,"

Adam stood up and kissed Jane. "They can't be that bad as I landed you,"

Henry smiled. It was great to see a couple in love, happy and just being a couple. Henry knew that Tom had wanted to hold his hands properly, he probably wanted to kiss him and he might have even wanted to have sex.

Henry never wanted to think about sex for now because it was too… awful. He wasn't a man down there and he just hated the idea of someone else seeing *that* awful part of him, but maybe he could at least let Tom kiss him.

He grinned at the idea. His stomach felt light and filled with butterflies. He really, really wanted to kiss Tom.

"Go on then," Jane said. "Get your shopping bags and then we can see what you bought Mister,"

Henry laughed and nodded as he hopped off the bar stool and went into the long dirty white corridor that led to the staircase. He really did love his friends and they were flat out amazing.

Henry was about to head up the steep staircase when someone knocked on the door. He had no idea who it could be at this hour. It would be too early for another of the housemates to be back from partying and it would be too late for someone to home round for a social call.

When the person started knocking again, Henry went to the large door and opened it.

He grinned as soon as he saw beautiful Tom standing there and then Tom just hugged him.

Henry loved it as he felt sheer attraction, chemistry and affection flow between them and Henry almost kissed Tom but then he noticed that Tom was angry.

"What's wrong?" Henry asked.

"Nothing, it's just my friends are dicks towards you,"

Henry took a few steps back. It was all happening again. Just like with his parents as soon as people found out he was trans they hated him, they despised him and they wanted him never to have existed.

It was the way the world worked.

"What happened?" Henry asked forcing himself not to react.

Tom threw his arms up in the air, shut the door

and he leant against a wall.

"I don't know me and my friends were having a great conversation. We were talking about partners and new girlfriends and boyfriends. They asked what your name was and then-"

Henry sighed as he knew that Tom had stopped because he realised how bad the thing was that his friend had said. It was too late. Henry knew exactly what he was going to say and it was the sad reality of life.

"Your friends think I am a girl, don't they?" Henry asked failing to hide the sadness in his voice.

"But I don't. I know you're a man, a really beautiful one,"

Henry moved away as Tom tried to hold his hand. He knew any relationship would be tough but he just didn't know it would be tough so soon.

"What happened next?"

"Henry it doesn't matter. I dealt with it,"

"What happened?" Henry asked firmly.

Tom shook his head and leant back against the wall. "We were arguing, Beth was defending you and I told my friends to *fuck off* and I hate them. They aren't my friends anymore,"

Henry hated this entire damn situation. He didn't want Henry to lose friends over him, Henry was nothing, he didn't want someone to dump friends for him. Henry was used to being abandoned and hated.

He didn't expect Tom to be any different.

"Don't lose friends over me," Henry said.

Tom laughed. "They aren't my friends. They aren't anything to me. I hate them,"

Henry took away a few more steps and then his phone buzzed. It was a text from his parents saying that they weren't going to pay for his accommodation next term but he could live with them with no judgement.

Henry bit his lower lip. It was a false promise because he actually didn't doubt the no judgement part but the accommodation contract was for all three terms and he had to pay at the beginning of each new term.

There were so many problems.

Henry hated how his parents were treating him. He hated that Tom was losing and fighting friends over him when he wasn't worth it. And Henry just hated that whatever happened the world would always hate him in return.

"I don't want to see you anymore," Henry said not daring to look at Tom. "I don't want you to lose friends over me. I don't want you to ruin your life because of me. I ruin everyone's life in the end. And just go and find a real man to be with,"

"But you are a real man," Tom said.

"Leave!" Henry shouted as he fought back tears. He had to spare Tom from a life of sadness, loneliness and hate. It was all Tom would get if he stayed with him.

And as Henry watched Tom frown and slam the door behind him he knew he had made a massive mistake.

But it was the only way to make sure Tom had the great life he really did deserve.

CHAPTER 13
22nd March 2023
Canterbury, England

After three long days, Tom was so annoyed at Jasmine and the others for being such dicks towards Henry. He had thankfully managed to avoid them in the kitchen, in the hallways and just avoided them period but he was so damn angry.

Tom didn't blame Henry at all for breaking up with him because it was down to Jasmine's abuse that made Henry stupidly believe that he was better off without it.

Tom flat out couldn't believe that his life would be better off without Henry, because Henry made him feel liked, alive and so damn light as he could float away whenever he was close to him. Tom loved Henry and it was just annoying that it had taken losing Henry to realise it.

"I was surprised it took you this long to call," Beth said holding two takeaway cups of coffee.

Tom weakly smiled as he sat down on a small wooden picnic table in the plaza of campus. There were tons of students going to class in their thick winter coats, trench coats and some were even wearing shorts. They were certainly the most adventurous of them all.

Tom smiled at Beth as she sat down next to him and he could just tell that she knew everything already.

"Let me guess," Tom said, "news gets round quickly in the queer grapevines,"

Beth laughed. "You could say that and yeah, I'm sorry about Henry dumping you. Do you believe me?"

Tom had no idea what she was talking about, she was the only person who had actually had the metaphorical balls to standup for Henry when all his "friends" decided that he wasn't right for being who he wanted to be.

"Believe me, you're the last person I would blame for what happened. It's all Jasmine's and those other idiot's fault," Tom said wrapping his hands tightly around the coffee cup.

Beth gestured they should walk and Tom rolled his eyes but nodded. He really didn't want to fight his way through the thousands of students coming and going from their lectures.

"What I didn't hear was why he dumped you?" Beth said nodding to one of her friends in the crowd.

Tom carefully stuck to the edges of the massive

river of students and shrugged. He didn't want to say the reasons aloud because they weren't real reasons, they were merely things that Henry had said to apparently protect him.

But he supposed if anyone could help him it was definitely going to be Beth.

"He said that he was ruining my life," Tom said. "He also said that he doesn't want me to lose friends over him and my personal favourite is he wants to meet a *real* man,"

"What bullshit," Beth said.

Tom laughed. "Exactly,"

He stepped to one side to get out of the massive river of students and he leant against a cold concrete wall and took a long boiling hot, bitter sip of the coffee.

Beth smiled next to him. "You know, the problem isn't you in the slightest. This is all about how Henry sees himself and all the life problems he has going on,"

Tom stood up perfectly straight. As much as he didn't want to believe it, he couldn't help but admit Beth sounded like she knew more than she was letting on.

"Go on," Tom said a little more forcefully than he intended.

"Fine, you know I do some part-time work in the University's financial support services,"

Tom nodded. That was a well-known fact that Beth had learnt very quickly to hide because tons of students started to ask her professional questions that she wasn't allowed to answer outside the office.

"Well, I've been talking to Henry for the past few days. Of course he doesn't know my surname so I doubt he's worked out who I am,"

Tom leant back against the icy coldness of the concrete wall. He held his stomach as he prepared himself for some kind of awful news.

"It turned out that his parents have decided to cut him off because he's trans. They want him to move back home but because of the way university accommodation leases work, he still needs to pay up,"

Tom shook his head and forced himself not to crush up the coffee cup in his hand. Not only because he didn't want to show how damn angry he was to Beth but also because he really didn't want boiling hot coffee over his hands.

"What can you do for him?" Tom asked.

Beth shrugged. "He has submitted an emergency loan and might be approved and I have given him the contact details of other people within my department but you're missing the point,"

Tom sighed. "Beth you know I love you but please cut to the chase,"

"It doesn't matter if Henry gets to stay in his shared house this term or any term after this one. He still doesn't believe anyone supports him and that he ruins lives,"

Tom shook his head. He so badly wanted to show Henry how amazing, wonderful and beautiful he was.

"And this is where I love you and leave you," Beth said, "because I have to go to work and then a lecture,"

"Wait," Tom said, "aren't you going to give me any details or anything? Aren't you meant to be the person to save this relationship?"

Beth laughed hard. A lot harder than Tom would have liked.

"I'm only telling you to get you started but try talking to Adam someone. I'll text you his name because he's a great friend of Henry's. Just convince Henry that you love him,"

Tom smiled as he hugged Beth and watched her walk away because she made it sound so damn easy. When in reality Tom just knew it really, really wasn't.

But he was going to give Henry his all.

CHAPTER 14
22nd March 2023
Canterbury, England

Henry knew he had absolutely fucked up the moment he had kicked the most wonderful man he had ever met out of his life. The past three days had been hell, lonely and damn annoying.

But as Henry laid on his cold soft bed in his shared house staring up at the ceiling, he supposed it was good that he was past the anger stage. He had already turned off his phone for the past three days and he had almost just been screaming and crying and swearing into his pillow.

But now he was just exhausted.

He was more than glad that the benefit of doing Outreach work was that he got to learn about all the different services the university offered, so he hoped he could get an emergency loan from the university that wouldn't charge him too much interest.

At least he still had a home to go back to next

term and then hopefully he would never have to go back to his parents' house.

Henry couldn't believe he had been so stupid as to let Tom go, the only man that ever truly believed in him, supported him and just wanted him to be happy. But Henry stood by his decisions, as painful and soul destroying as it was he didn't want Tom to lose his friends and to be dragged down by him.

It was that simple.

Henry rolled over and buried his head in the pillow. His laptop was over on the desk and he really wanted the university to email him back about his loan and then his laptop's ringtone flared to life.

Henry forced himself up in case it was the damn university, he forced himself over to his black desk chair and he answered it.

"Uncle Henry!" Daniel shouted.

Henry instantly sat up straight and he almost cried at the beautiful sight of his little nephew on his mother's laptop.

"Hi buddy, what's up?"

"Mummy says I can use the lappy top for ma homework. I wanted to call you because Mean Nanny doesn't let me. Why doesn't Nanny like you?"

Henry fought back tears. He loved his family so much and he wanted to see his precious nephew more, he wanted to see his brother and sister more and he just wanted a family again.

"Because Dan," Henry said, "because she gets angry about some stuff but it doesn't matter. She loves you and that's all that matters,"

"But I want to play trains with you. Mummy bought me a massive choo-choo train last Sunday. She's working and Daddy's sleeping cos he's lazy I have no one to play with,"

Henry laughed. "Buddy, your daddy isn't lazy. He needs to work when you're asleep so Mummy can keep buying you your trains,"

Henry loved it when Daniel gave him a very questioning look. "So Daddy isn't abandoning me and Mummy and isn't a bad Daddy?"

Henry shook his head. "No, your Daddy loves you. He works so much so he can give you all the trains he can,"

Daniel gave him a very slow nod. "Nanny's silly isn't she for saying that,"

Henry nodded.

"Hey little man," Henry's sister said as she popped into the camera view. "How about you get a drink and I promise you you can talk to Uncle Henry in a minute?"

"You promise mummy? Not a Nanny promise?" Daniel said.

Henry forced himself to keep smiling as Daniel was looking between him and his sister. Henry hated how the sweat rolled down his back and his heart pounded in his chest as Sophie hugged Daniel and little Daniel ran off.

Henry gulped as soon as Sophie sat down.

"I promise I didn't contact him," Henry said. "I

know I'm not allowed,"

Sophie rolled her eyes. "Thanks for saying that to him about his Dad. I know it annoys Danny more than anyone knows,"

"How is he?" Henry asked, knowing him and Sophie rarely spoke about anything.

"He's working a lot. He just wants to give Dan a childhood like he never had, so thanks for showing Dan that he's a good dad,"

"Anytime," Henry said. "Did you want to never call again?"

"Sod off," Sophie said smiling. "I've never had a problem with having two brothers. It means more make-up for me and I'm still using up all your crap,"

Henry laughed. He had always hated his family buying him make-up and other girly things when he was a teenager so he had forced it on poor Sophie.

"I miss this," Henry said, "why didn't we stay in touch?"

"Oh you know, life, I have a kid and let's say it mum is a bitch,"

"Amen to that," Henry said as he took a deep breath. "Did you hear what Mum did about my accommodation?"

"If it changes anything I did shout at her, I promise. It isn't right what she convinced Dad to do but you know, he never had a backbone in the first place. You will come here, right if you need to?"

"I'll take you up on that probably," Henry said smiling. He would love to stay with Sophie, Daniel and her husband.

"I also heard about you have a boyfriend,"

"I ruined it all. I broke up with him because he deserves a better life. How can I give him anything if everyone hates me, none of his friends like trans people and I just ruin everyone's lives, like yours,"

"How?" Sophia asked like that was the most stupidest thing she had ever heard.

"You argued with Mum over me. I've damaged your relationships and I just cause so much drama,"

"What's drama Uncle Henry?" Daniel said as he climbed up on Sophie's lap.

Henry laughed as Sophie kissed Daniel on the forehead.

"Danny, tell Uncle Henry what you said to me last night about him,"

"I want to see Uncle Henry most because I love him and he's fun to play with. He gets trains and he lets me play past my bedtime. When can he come round again?"

Henry forced himself not to cry.

"You never ruin lives baby bro," Sophie said, "and let me just say you are a much better *brother* than a *sister*. You were a shit sister,"

Henry laughed and blew them both a kiss and he and Sophie promised Daniel that he would come round soon so they could play trains together.

Henry collapsed onto the bed and just let it all out because that was the nicest conversation he had had with his family in a long long time.

Now he just needed to fix everything in his relationship. Something he had no idea how to do.

Not an idea at all.

CHAPTER 15
23rd March 2023
Canterbury, England

Tom flat out couldn't believe how hard it had been to track down Adam even after Beth had sent him his full name. Tom had even visited Kent University's physics society to try and find Adam last night but that really hadn't worked.

Tom had searched the campus, library but now he was really hoping he had found Adam because he could have sworn that Adam was playing football for the university team about a mile away from campus.

Tom leant against a very cold, bumpy and slightly sticky silver birch tree right next to the path that led back to the university. As he watched the entire university football team pack up, finish their cool down and then manly hug each other. Which was something else that Tom didn't understand about homophobia in football. All these footballers in tight shorts hugging each other seriously looked gay.

A lot gayer than Tom did.

After a moment Tom saw a man that matched Adam's description and he called him over.

"Yes?" Adam asked. "Who are you?"

"Tom," he said. "I'm a friend of Henry and that's what I want to talk to you about please,"

Adam laughed and gestured they should walk and talk. Tom forced himself not to gag at the strong overwhelming smell of manly musk, sweat and mud that invaded his senses as him and Adam walked up the long concrete path back towards the university.

"From what I hear you two aren't friends anymore which is a shame," Adam said, "and come on, I don't know you,"

"But you must know that he really liked me and I liked him back," Tom said not knowing what his guy's problem was.

"True but given how awful his parents are, *your* friends were and how much I want to protect Henry, why should I help you?"

Tom stopped and nodded. He could see where Adam was coming from. It was clear that he liked Henry a lot and he only wanted to protect his friend and Tom had no idea what Henry had told Adam but Tom just wanted Adam to know that he wasn't the danger here.

"I haven't spoken to those idiots for days and they aren't my friends," Tom said. "They stopped being my friends the moment they called Henry a woman,"

Adam shook his head. "That's fucking sick and come on, does it actually matter if someone wants to be a man or woman. All these transphobes are going to wake up tomorrow and their life isn't going to be any different or worse off for seeing a trans person,"

"Exactly," Tom said liking how much Adam cared about Henry.

"I'm sorry how I was earlier. It's just that I've known Henry a long time and I never like seeing him get hurt and he doesn't believe anything anyone ever says about him. At least the nice stuff,"

Tom nodded. As much as he hated the confirmation bias where people blocked out all information that didn't support their beliefs and attitudes, he could really understand why Henry had fallen for it.

Tom understood why Henry had negative beliefs about being trans and why he might never be accepted, able to pass or he would improve people's lives but Tom just wanted Henry to know he was loved.

So damn much.

"And it's annoying that Henry's sealed himself away from everyone for the past three days,"

Tom shook his head. That really was the last thing that Henry needed. Henry needed to be around people that loved him, supported him and appreciated him for being him.

Henry didn't need to be alone.

Tom looked at Adam. "What do you think I need

to do?"

"You need," Adam said, "just to show him that you don't care about the hate, the comments or anything. You need to show him that you don't give a damn about him being trans that you love him. Do you love him?"

"Yes," Tom said out of instinct and he loved how it wasn't forced, strangled or anything. He had said it because it was the truth.

And Tom smiled because something clicked inside him and he felt amazing, hopeful and the lightest he ever felt before.

Tom knew he had always been slightly weary of his gay side. He had always been curious, unsure and even avoiding dating because he didn't know what others would say, who would want him and he supposed that life was just simpler if he appeared straight without a relationship.

At least that way his wider family wouldn't find out and then they wouldn't judge and his parents would keep off his back.

All those feelings and fears had been buried for so long that Tom didn't know they were even there. But right now as he looked at Adam, he realised that he had needed to accept a few things about himself and he was okay now.

He was happily gay, he was going to have a boyfriend and they were going to date. That was perfectly okay and Tom couldn't help but smile as he couldn't believe how right, natural and perfect that felt.

He was gay and going to have a boyfriend if everything went to plan.

A plan he still needed to think of and actually do.

CHAPTER 16
24th March 2023
Canterbury, England

Henry was so damn happy with himself after the past two wonderful days of becoming more confident, accepting himself more and he had been pushing himself more and more into doing things he never ever would have considered doing before. He had gone into a public male toilet (something he only did when he was dying for a wee before), he had gone clothes shopping again in a Male-Only store and he had had some great conversations about sports with some random strangers at a sports bar.

He was really grateful his sister had given him a bunch of conversation tips beforehand. And he loved it how everyone hadn't noticed he was trans or most importantly (and probably) not a single person had given a shit about him.

"Being a man is brilliant," Henry said as he sat around the large kitchen island in his shared kitchen with Jane, Jordan and Adam sitting around it with large mugs of hot chocolate as all the other housemates were out at a party tonight.

Henry was really glad that his best friends had all wanted to see him instead of going to the major party, and he absolutely loved them for it.

Jane and Adam were hugging and had their arms loosely wrapped round each other as they drank their hot chocolate, and Henry was so glad to see all of them. Because he was really hoping they were going to help him deal with the last source of pain in his life.

He had to deal with his mother but he wanted to ease into that topic with his friends first.

"You know," Adam said, "your boyfriend came to see me yesterday. He wanted to know how to make stuff right and everything,"

Henry grinned. It felt amazing to know that beautiful, sexy Tom still cared about him so maybe there was a way he could fix it all.

"I told him he needed to show you that he loved you and that he didn't care that you were trans," Adam said.

Henry couldn't disagree because even though he was pushing himself more and more in the past few days maybe he did need someone else to confirm everything to him.

"Thanks for that," Henry said. "I've been trying a lot to accept myself,"

"I did tell you were a beautiful man," Adam said,

"but I guess that's different from a gay guy telling it to you,"

Henry nodded. "That was why I loved spending time with Tom. My beautiful, beautiful Tom that I have to fix everything with but I want your help,"

"Anything mate," Jordan said.

Henry took a deep breath of the sweet chocolate-scented air. "I want you guys to be in the video call with my mother so she can see that not everyone hates me for being trans,"

He was surprised when Jane, Adam and Jordan nodded and smiled without even looking at each other.

"Thanks," Henry said taking out his phone and video-calling his mother.

As it started dialling all his best friends gathered around him and they smiled, and Henry was a little surprised that his mother didn't decline the call straight away.

She answered it.

"Hey mum," Henry said.

"Why are you calling? Do you know how much trouble you're in? Calling your sister and influencing-"

"Be quiet mate," Jordan said. "Your son is an amazing *man* that is nice, kind and the bestest friend I could have asked for. And he is so much nicer than you will ever be,"

"Exactly," Adam said. "Me and my girlfriend are lucky to have *him* in our lives. He is always happy to help us with physics, he is supportive and I'm sorry but from everything I know about your husband. Your *son* is more of a man than he will ever be,"

Henry laughed at that.

Just before his mother could start talking again, Jane spoke up after kissing Henry on the head.

"And your *son* is funny, kind and a great dresser. I don't know why you would not have a relationship with him because he is excellent. And the world would be a poorer place without this *man* in it,"

"So take that mum," Henry said.

His mother frowned and Henry could see that she wasn't sure what to do. She actually looked scared for the first time in her life and Henry realised this was probably the first time anyone had ever stuck up to her. His father never had, his brother and his sister never really did.

And Henry had always been focusing on survival and hating himself too much to stand up to his mother.

"I know this is difficult mother for you to understand," Henry said. "But I am Henry, I am your son and I will always love you but unless you want to start trying to be nice to me. Then I don't want to see you again,"

Henry forced himself not to react as his mother started tearing up. It was the least she deserved and Henry couldn't have cared less about his mother's feelings, not after the years of everything she had done to him.

"Fine then," his mother said. "I will try,"

"I will try, who?" Adam said.

His mother laughed. "I will try *Henry*,"

"Thank you mum. I mean it,"

His mother weakly smiled and then Henry ended the video call and he just grinned at his friends because he finally had his parents back and he knew it would be a long road to recovery, to a point where they could actually be mother, father and son instead of mother, father and the failure. But Henry was okay with that because there was a hope and a chance of acceptance.

Something he always wanted and now he just needed to fix his relationship with the man he loved.

Something that was going to get a hell of a lot easier as Henry's phone buzzed in his hand.

CHAPTER 17
24th March 2023
Canterbury, England

Henry leant against the icy coldness of the silver birch tree in the middle of the massive university field on the other side of campus from his shared house. The night was cold and fresh, the air was damp with hints of freshly cut grass in it and the air had a minor bite that made Henry really wish that Tom would hurry up and turn up.

Henry really liked how there was no one else on the field. There might have been a few shadows up in the distance near the university buildings but they were far away and soon the man he loved would be here.

He had loved talking to Tom on the phone and then Henry had checked out Tom's social media. Henry had almost cried about the posts about how Tom supported trans people unconditionally that there was nothing wrong with loving them and that ultimately trans men were men and transwomen were women. Because this wasn't a choice, it was just a part of who they were.

Henry couldn't agree more strongly with that.

He felt so light, airy and alive as he stood under the silver birch tree. And he noticed for the first time ever, there was an absence of something inside him.

He didn't know if it was a lack of fear, a lack of hate or a lack of shame that he felt about being trans or gay. He just didn't know but whatever it was he was so glad that he felt so much lighter, happier and he really wanted to kiss the beautiful man he loved.

"I haven't seen you here before," Tom said grinning like a little schoolboy as he came over.

Henry laughed and just grabbed him. Pulling beautiful Tom close and Henry just savoured Tom's slightly manly musky scent, his wonderful earthy aftershave and just the wonderful feeling of his body warmth against his own.

"I'm so sorry," Henry said pulling wonderful Tom even closer.

"You don't need to apologise for anything because, I'm not friends with any of those people anymore. I meant what I said on my social media. I couldn't give a rat's behind about what you were at birth,"

Henry took Tom's soft hands in his.

"You're a man now and you're a really, really beautiful man," Tom said, "and I never want you to be alone again,"

"Will you have me back?" Henry asked knowing the answer was a given.

"I wouldn't be here if I didn't want you as my boyfriend," Tom said knowing Henry knew the answer, "I could be working on a psychology assignment but I would much rather be here with you,"

Henry looked at Tom's soft, beautiful, perfect lips. They were so smooth, so manly, so tasty that all Henry wanted, needed to do was kiss them but he had never kissed another guy before.

"Can I, you know, kiss you?" Henry asked like a little teenager out on his first date.

"You never need to ask," Tom said as he pressed his perfect lips against Henry's.

Henry gasped and moaned at the sheer tenderness, passion and emotion behind the kiss. This wasn't a careless, sloppy kiss that meant nothing.

This was a kiss that Tom was using to make sure that Henry knew, truly knew that he loved him, cared about him and never ever wanted to be away from Henry ever again. And if that mind-blowing kiss was anything to go by then Henry was seriously never going to let him go again.

"I do love you Tom," Henry said. "I mean it because for the first time ever I feel like I actually know who I am and that's a great thing to know,"

"I'm glad because I love you too Henry,"

Henry kissed his wonderful boyfriend again and again and then when Tom pushed him up against the rough bark of the silver birch tree he was surprised that he didn't stop it. Even before he knew that nothing was going to happen.

And as Tom whispered sexy, adult and wonderful things in his ear about what he wanted to do to Henry, Henry just grinned because he finally wanted to have sex, he finally wanted to have a boyfriend, he finally wanted to have it all.

And Henry realised that he had been right earlier, he felt so much lighter, happier and the best he had in years because he simply didn't feel shame, hate or fear about being who he was.

He had accepted himself and Henry had to admit that was an amazing thing to feel after so many years of hate. And that was all because of the wonderful, beautiful man he was kissing.

Something Henry didn't want to stop doing any time soon.

CHAPTER 18
4th March 2024
Canterbury, England

"Uncle Tom!"

Tom laughed as he went into the massive living room that belonged to Sophie and her husband filled with great artwork, massive blue fabric sofas and most importantly the most precious little nephew Tom had ever had.

Tom sat down on the wonderfully soft sofa as Daniel ran over to him and started telling him all sorts of things about school, his parents and all the really cool things he had been doing lately. He might have only been 5 years old but Tom was still amazed how long Daniel could talk for.

He smiled as Sophie and her husband went to the front door to talk and help beautiful Henry bring in Daniel's birthday presents as they were going away at the week of his real birthday to celebrate their one year anniversary together.

As Daniel kept talking more and more about his amazing dino collection, Tom just smiled and nodded and realised that he loved his life. Sure Sophie's living room was covered in artwork he never would have chosen, it was filled with the scents of limes, lemons and grapefruits that somehow worked together, but Tom loved how this entire living room was dedicated to family.

In amongst all the artwork, Tom loved looking at all the photos framed in gold of him and Henry making out at the New Year's party, there were photos of him, Henry and Daniel laughing when Tom finally convinced everyone that a picnic would be a great idea. And there were just so many great memories on the walls.

And Tom loved his new family and he loved Henry even more. It was great that Henry and his parents were getting on better, they still sometimes called him Harriet by mistake but it was always an honest mistake and they always gave him twenty pounds as a massive "I'm sorry".

Tom didn't mind too much because they were trying, learning and their mistakes alone had paid for him and Henry to go abroad in July for a wonderful holiday together.

"Uncle Henry!" Daniel said jumping off Tom's lap.

Daniel ran over to Henry and hugged him and then immediately started repeating himself to Henry. Tom was starting to really hope that he didn't already have all the toys they had bought him for his birthday.

"Hey little man," Sophie said. "Why don't you go and get your really cool drawing of Uncle Henry and Tom that you did at school?"

"Okay mummy," Daniel said running off.

"He's been dying to show you both it," Sophie said grinning.

Tom looked at the beautiful man he loved as Henry came over and sat next to him. Tom kissed his soft beautiful lips and almost hissed as he caught himself on some of Henry's beard that was slowly growing.

"But we have a surprise you for," Sophie said gesturing to her husband to get something.

Tom hugged Henry as Sophie's husband (the very definition of a macho guy) came back into the living room with a massive black bag from a department store that Tom didn't recognise.

"Every real man needs one of these," Sophie's husband said to Henry. "Or to at least try it once,"

Tom looked at beautiful Henry as he got out the gift certificates for the four of them to go rally car driving. And Tom really wanted to be sick but then he saw how much Henry, Sophie and her husband were smiling and he could tell that this was exactly what the three of them had always wanted.

Tom didn't really know too much about their relationship before they had started to repair things close to a year ago, but Tom could tell that they loved each other and wanted to spend more time together.

And if that meant putting up with the hell of a rally car driving experience then Tom supposed that he would have to manage.

"Uncles!" Daniel said racing back into the living room and he gave Tom his drawing.

Tom had no idea at all what he was looking at. As far as he was concerned it was all lines and colours and lovely little messages in a weird alien handwriting that he didn't understand. But he loved Daniel and considering this precious little five-year-old had kickstarted everything that had gotten their relationship back together, Tom was only ever going to show Daniel the love he deserved.

"It looks amazing," Tom said.

"Really?" Daniel asked.

"Sure thing buddy," Henry said.

Daniel took it off them and then ran back upstairs laughing and screaming all like overexcited children do and then Tom just kissed Henry on the lips.

"What was that for?" Henry asked.

"Because I love you. I love your family and I love that we get to be together and I love you even more for being who you are," Tom said. "I love you for being a beautiful man that I will always treasure, love and adore,"

Henry smiled. "And I love you for accepting me and for some reason, I don't think we'll be breaking up for a long, long time,"

"Try never," Tom said as the two of them

laughed and kissed again and then Sophie and her husband joined in the hug and then little Daniel joined in too.

This was the meaning of family and love and Tom was so glad he got to be a part of it with the man he would always love until the end of time.

ACCEPTING LOVE

GET YOUR FREE SHORT STORY NOW!

And get signed up to Connor Whiteley's newsletter to hear about new gripping books, offers and exciting projects. (You'll never be sent spam)

https://www.subscribepage.com/gayromancesignup

About the author:

Connor Whiteley is the author of over 60 books in the sci-fi fantasy, nonfiction psychology and books for writer's genre and he is a Human Branding Speaker and Consultant.

He is a passionate warhammer 40,000 reader, psychology student and author.

Who narrates his own audiobooks and he hosts The Psychology World Podcast.

All whilst studying Psychology at the University of Kent, England.

Also, he was a former Explorer Scout where he gave a speech to the Maltese President in August 2018 and he attended Prince Charles' 70th Birthday Party at Buckingham Palace in May 2018.

Plus, he is a self-confessed coffee lover!

Other books by Connor Whiteley:

Bettie English Private Eye Series

A Very Private Woman

The Russian Case

A Very Urgent Matter

A Case Most Personal

Trains, Scots and Private Eyes

The Federation Protects

Cops, Robbers and Private Eyes

Just Ask Bettie English

An Inheritance To Die For

The Death of Graham Adams

Bearing Witness

The Twelve

The Wrong Body

The Assassination Of Bettie English

Wining And Dying

Eight Hours

Uniformed Cabal

A Case Most Christmas

Gay Romance Novellas

Breaking, Nursing, Repairing A Broken Heart

Jacob And Daniel

Fallen For A Lie

Spying And Weddings

Clean Break

Awakening Love
Meeting A Country Man
Loving Prime Minister
Snowed In Love
Never Been Kissed
Love Betrays You

Lord of War Origin Trilogy:
Not Scared Of The Dark
Madness
Burn Them All

The Fireheart Fantasy Series
Heart of Fire
Heart of Lies
Heart of Prophecy
Heart of Bones
Heart of Fate

City of Assassins (Urban Fantasy)
City of Death
City of Marytrs
City of Pleasure
City of Power

Agents of The Emperor
Return of The Ancient Ones
Vigilance
Angels of Fire
Kingmaker
The Eight
The Lost Generation
Hunt
Emperor's Council
Speaker of Treachery
Birth Of The Empire
Terraforma
Spaceguard

The Rising Augusta Fantasy Adventure Series
Rise To Power
Rising Walls
Rising Force
Rising Realm

Lord Of War Trilogy (Agents of The Emperor)
Not Scared Of The Dark
Madness
Burn It All Down

Miscellaneous:
RETURN
FREEDOM
SALVATION
Reflection of Mount Flame
The Masked One
The Great Deer
English Independence

OTHER SHORT STORIES BY CONNOR WHITELEY

Mystery Short Story Collections
Criminally Good Stories Volume 1: 20 Detective Mystery Short Stories
Criminally Good Stories Volume 2: 20 Private Investigator Short Stories
Criminally Good Stories Volume 3: 20 Crime Fiction Short Stories
Criminally Good Stories Volume 4: 20 Science Fiction and Fantasy Mystery Short Stories
Criminally Good Stories Volume 5: 20 Romantic Suspense Short Stories

Mystery Short Stories:
Protecting The Woman She Hated
Finding A Royal Friend

ACCEPTING LOVE

Our Woman In Paris
Corrupt Driving
A Prime Assassination
Jubilee Thief
Jubilee, Terror, Celebrations
Negative Jubilation
Ghostly Jubilation
Killing For Womenkind
A Snowy Death
Miracle Of Death
A Spy In Rome
The 12:30 To St Pancreas
A Country In Trouble
A Smokey Way To Go
A Spicy Way To GO
A Marketing Way To Go
A Missing Way To Go
A Showering Way To Go
Poison In The Candy Cane
Kendra Detective Mystery Collection Volume 1
Kendra Detective Mystery Collection Volume 2
Mystery Short Story Collection Volume 1
Mystery Short Story Collection Volume 2
Criminal Performance
Candy Detectives

Key To Birth In The Past

<u>Fantasy Short Stories:</u>
City of Snow
City of Light
City of Vengeance
Dragons, Goats and Kingdom
Smog The Pathetic Dragon
Don't Go In The Shed
The Tomato Saver
The Remarkable Way She Died
Dragon Coins
Dragon Tea
Dragon Rider

<u>All books in 'An Introductory Series':</u>
Careers In Psychology
Psychology of Suicide
Dementia Psychology
Clinical Psychology Reflections Volume 4
Forensic Psychology of Terrorism And Hostage-Taking
Forensic Psychology of False Allegations
Year In Psychology
CBT For Anxiety
CBT For Depression
Applied Psychology

ACCEPTING LOVE

BIOLOGICAL PSYCHOLOGY 3RD EDITION
COGNITIVE PSYCHOLOGY THIRD EDITION
SOCIAL PSYCHOLOGY- 3RD EDITION
ABNORMAL PSYCHOLOGY 3RD EDITION
PSYCHOLOGY OF RELATIONSHIPS- 3RD EDITION
DEVELOPMENTAL PSYCHOLOGY 3RD EDITION
HEALTH PSYCHOLOGY
RESEARCH IN PSYCHOLOGY
A GUIDE TO MENTAL HEALTH AND TREATMENT AROUND THE WORLD- A GLOBAL LOOK AT DEPRESSION
FORENSIC PSYCHOLOGY
THE FORENSIC PSYCHOLOGY OF THEFT, BURGLARY AND OTHER CRIMES AGAINST PROPERTY
CRIMINAL PROFILING: A FORENSIC PSYCHOLOGY GUIDE TO FBI PROFILING AND GEOGRAPHICAL AND STATISTICAL PROFILING.
CLINICAL PSYCHOLOGY
FORMULATION IN PSYCHOTHERAPY
PERSONALITY PSYCHOLOGY AND

CONNOR WHITELEY

INDIVIDUAL DIFFERENCES CLINICAL PSYCHOLOGY REFLECTIONS VOLUME 1
CLINICAL PSYCHOLOGY REFLECTIONS VOLUME 2
Clinical Psychology Reflections Volume 3
CULT PSYCHOLOGY
Police Psychology

A Psychology Student's Guide To University
How Does University Work?
A Student's Guide To University And Learning
University Mental Health and Mindset

www.ingramcontent.com/pod-product-compliance
Lightning Source LLC
LaVergne TN
LVHW012120070526
838202LV00056B/5799